Drabble Harvest: Interstellar Archives

Edited by Terrie Leigh Relf

DRABBLE HARVEST IS EDITED BY
TERRIE LEIGH RELF

All rights reserved. No part of this book may be reproduced or transmitted in any form or by any means, electronic or mechanical, including photo-copying or recording or by any information storage and retrieval systems, without expressed written consent of the author and/or artists. Any similarity between places and persons mentioned in the fiction or semi-fiction and real places or persons living or dead is coincidental.

Story copyrights owned by the respective authors

Cover Art "A Proper Library" and cover design by Laura Givens

Drabble Harvest is published twice a year, in conjunction with The Hiraeth Publishing Drabble Contests

Contents

34 First Place: Banned Books by Keith Burdon
25 Second Place: Omega by Anthony Perconti
23 Honorable Mention: Foreign Discoveries by Sara Kate Egan
29 Honorable Mention: Among the Rain Readers by Tom Gadd

5 A Little Help, Please
10 Editorial by Terrie Leigh Relf
12 Grieving Tonic by Amber Sayer
13 Curiosity by Lisa Timpf
14 Weeding by Amber Tacey
15 Don't Worry, You'll Have Plenty of Time to Read All of the Books by Francis W. Alexander
19 Welcome to the Archive by Taria Karillion
22 Answered Call by Tom Duke
32 Galactic Emperor Library 45 by Art Gomez
33 Not Fit for Public Consumption by Lee Clark Zumpe
37 Widely Read by Greg Schwartz
38 Far From Home by Nina D'Arcangela
40 Return to Archives by Gary Davis

SALE AT HIRAETH PUBLISHING!!!

THERE'S A SALE GOING ON!!! IT'S STILL GOING ON!!!

BUY ALL THE BOOKS YOU WANT AND USE THIS 20% DISCOUNT CODE: **BOOKS2024)**

GO TO OUR SHOP AT WWW.HIRAETHSFFH.COM

NO MASKS, NO WAITING, AND WE NEVER CLOSE!

From the desk of the deputy assistant adjutant to the Boortean Ambassador

A Little Help, Please

In the world of the small indie press we fight a never-ending battle for attention to our work, as writers and in publishing. Here's an example: big publishers [you know who they are] have gobs of $$$ that they can devote to advertising and marketing. Here at Hiraeth Publishing, our advertising budget consists of the deposits for whatever soda bottles and aluminum cans we can find alongside the highways. Anti-littering laws make our task even more difficult . . . ☺

That's where YOU come in. YOU are our best promoter. YOU are the one who can tell others about us. Just send 'em to our website, tell them about our store. That's all. Just that.

Of course, we don't mind if you talk us up. We're pretty good, you know. We have some award-winning and award-nominated writers and artists, plus other voices well-deserving to be heard [not everyone wins awards, right?] but our publications are read-worthy nevertheless.

That number once again is:

www.hiraethsffh.com

Friend us on Facebook at Hiraeth Publish

Follow us on Twitter at @HiraethPublish1

Iuliae: Past Tense
By Tyree Campbell

Two sisters of the Iulius Family have run away from the restrictions and rules of their settlement on a remote world, and embark on a journey of discovery, to learn what to do with their new-found freedom. Along the way, they become smugglers, and opponents of human trafficking, and become fugitives from the law and from the corporations.

Iulia Sexta, the younger of the two sisters, is suffering from an identity crisis. Is it gender dysphoria? Was she supposed to be a man? Is that why she likes girls? Or is a ghost from one of her previous lives now trying to haunt his way back into the living by taking over her body and mind?

With both the past and the present pursuing them, Iulia Tertia and Iulia Sexta find their future under constant attack. Doing the right thing is not only difficult at best, but may well result in their deaths. What to do? One thing at a time...

Order and read the adventure of a lifetime!

https://www.hiraethsffh.com/product-page/iuliae-past-tense-by-tyree-campbell

The Sisterhood of the Blood Moon
By Terrie Leigh Relf

For thousands of Earth years, the Transgalactic Consortium has had an invested interest in this planet and its inhabitants, the Haurans. While the Sisterhood of the Blood Moon and the Guardians work together with the Consortium and Haurans to restore balance to the universe, the Blood Moon is fast approaching. The power of this moon reveals untold secrets . . . including the sacred covenant with the Mora Spiders. There is an ancient pact that continues to be honored – but at what cost and for whose purpose?

The world may come to an end. But will there be a chance for a new beginning? And if so, where?

Find out! Order a copy now!

https://www.hiraethsffh.com/product-page/sisterhood-of-the-blood-moon-by-terrie-leigh-relf

Interstellar Archives Drabbler

Greetings Interstellar Travelers, Haurans, and Friends of Boort:

Let us give thanks for archivists, curators, historians, librarians, scribes, writers— and other service-oriented beings (unless they are attempting to ban or otherwise condemn tomes and other treasure troves of knowledge). As you will discover by reading this brief report, there are individuals throughout the galaxy who are attempting to preserve knowledge while other factions are attempting to destroy it. Be vigilant when faced with those whose synapses are not firing in the correct direction.

Your humble ambassador,
Terrie Leigh Relf

https://www.hiraethsffh.com/product-page/woman-from-the-institute-by-tyree-campbell

Grieving Tonic
Amber Sayer

Kadex hadn't visited the Memorium in years. He hadn't needed to. Losing her changed everything.

Hovering over a large crater, the Memorium stood tall and proud, crafted from incandescent light, not solid materials.

Kadex entered, jumping through a ripple of immodest green rays.

Inside, the eerie glow illuminated shimmering archives of his people's memories projected as holographic images.

Kadex wanted to investigate the new collections featured in the atrium.

But not today.

Today, there was just one stack he needed. A folio of holograms flashed magenta.

"I miss you, Mom."

"I know, sweetie. You're grieving. Come relive our memories together."

Curiosity
Lisa Timpf

Morgana snorted as she skulked through the space station housing the Interstellar Archives. That disposal chute she'd spotted indicated the station still used an onboard incinerator instead of nuclear power.

She thought the Greenoans, who traveled space before humans painted on cave walls, would be more technically advanced. If their surveillance tech was at the same level, she'd have no problem accessing the forbidden files.

* * *

The Curator stiffened when she heard the alarm. The video feed showed a human attempting to access the Vault.

Good thing they still had the onboard incinerator. It came in handy for cases like this . . .

Weeding
Amber Tacey

"How many worlds are archived? We only have room for so many. This looks cluttered. This weeding project should be much farther along."

Arnest tucked two more marble-sized worlds into his sleeve as he trailed behind the Senior Archivist. He couldn't bear to obliterate entire worlds of knowledge just because others thought they were obsolete.

"Are you listening, Arnest? I feel that your mind is elsewhere."

"I'm sorry, your Knowledgeness." Arnest pretended to straighten his hair, tucking a pea-sized planet into the whorl of his left ear for safe keeping. How many he could smuggle out of the archive today?

Don't Worry, You'll Have Plenty of Time to Read All of the Books
Francis W. Alexander

"Come," the cat says.

I follow. This is some kind of stack area of a library.

Through my mind's eye, I see countless floors, aisles, and shelves. It reminds me of the movie *Interstellar,* but it is much larger.

"Here, a minute is one hundred years. So read to your heart's content."

Stepping into an aisle, the first book I see is *The Intergalactic Cookbook* by Marge Simon, Sandy DeLuca, and Terrie Relf.

Something pulls me out of the room, through a tunnel, and into a light. I open my eyes.

"We thought we lost you," Hospice Nurse Becky says.

The Red Foil
t.santitoro

When Soefee Sparrow's roommate and ex-lover, Tayla Block, goes missing aboard a space mining station, Sparrow—a rocket-horse jockey—suddenly finds herself under suspicion of murder.

Despite the mining company's main source of income—megatons of industrial minerals and gem stones—no one but Soefee seems to be searching for their leading geologist.

Were gemstones being stolen from the mining company? Did it have anything to do with Block's disappearance? Why was everyone being so tight-lipped?

What happened to Tayla Block, and why wasn't anything being done to find her?

Enter Jicob Elfrendini, an undercover agent for IBCP, a division of Law Enforcement employed to ensure against the theft of valuable gems. But Elfrendini has secrets of his own.

And then a woman's dead body is found at the bottom of a mine shaft and, together, Soefee and Jicob must work to find out who killed Tayla Block—

--and WHY?

Ordering Links
Print: https://www.hiraethsffh.com/product-page/red-foil-by-t-santitoro
ePub: https://www.hiraethsffh.com/product-page/red-foil-by-t-santitoro-2
PDF: https://www.hiraethsffh.com/product-page/red-foil-by-t-santitoro-1

And NOW a word from one of our new sponsors . . .
(Brought to YOU by the Boortean Ambassador)

Tertu's Trans-Stellar Writing Retreat

Have you fantasized about being far away from your usual activities so that you can focus on your writing? Would you like to be surrounded by poets and tale tellers from throughout your galaxy and beyond? Then sign up NOW for this amazing opportunity! Not only will there be daily prompts, open mic nights, guest speakers, and other writerly activities aboard our trans-galactic vacation cruiser, just imagine having access to an interstellar library! We have portal access to some of the best curated libraries in the universe! Contact us NOW to learn more and sign up for this stellar experience!

Welcome to The Archive
Taria Karillion

Welcome to this Interstellar Archive pod. Please place your DNA sample into the scanner.

ADVISORY
- A slight tingling from the connector pads is normal. Please refrain from placing them on sensitive body areas. We are not liable for any injury, trauma or bodily effects resulting from use of this service (including, but not limited to, the following: rashes, fever, flatulence, appearance and/or disappearance of limbs, hallucinations or pregnancy.)
- For beings accessing data on the planet Sol 3/Earth, our sincere condolences. We offer post-consultation counselling for guilt, paranoia and anger management. Tissues, mops and memory wipes are also accessible below.

Loading . . .

Adopted Child
By Teri Santitoro
(aka sakyu)

Imp, now 13, has awakened from stasis by MA, the ship's computer, to find that everyone else has been killed by a highly infectious disease. She is alone on the ship. But she is about to have visitors.

The *Greentown*, a salvage ship, has spotted a derelict and is about to board her for salvage rights. The crew is blissfully unaware of what happened to the people on the derelict. Soon enough they will find out...but will it be too late? And what of the girl who now controls the derelict?

To everyone involved, everything is new...and potentially lethal.

Ordering Links:
Print Edition:
https://www.hiraethsffh.com/product-page/adopted-child-by-t-santitoro

PDF Edition:
https://www.hiraethsffh.com/product-page/adopted-child-by-t-santitoro-1

Answered Call
(From the journal of Spytz, the Gypsy Cat Space Ghost)
Tom Duke

Have I mentioned I was once a Library Cat? My hangout was the Archives section of a global space-exploration group dedicated to searching for alien life (like SETI, only secret). I know things only a select few people and no other cats that I'm aware of know. In 1974, the Arecibo Radio Telescope in Puerto Rico beamed the strongest signal ever into outer-space announcing our existence (common knowledge). But now, fifty years later, we've heard back (secret). The source is twenty-five light years away. You wonder if they're coming and how long it will take?

You should be wondering "why?"

Honorable Mention

Foreign Discoveries
Sara Kate Egan

"Sure is dusty in here," I remark, gasping for air.

My boss, Noelle, and I are assigned to investigate the old library of capital city Lionessa. Now a ghost town, on an abandoned planet, we're searching through records for intel.

"Noelle, look!" I'm intrigued. Thousands of names and dates fill a gigantic, green book. Some are famous, but two of utmost familiarity jump out.

"What's this list for?" With concern, I inquire. Not disclosing my parents' names or birthdates being shown.

She hesitates, then hushedly reveals. "Our theory is they've all left for Earth, disguised as humans before taking over."

And NOW a word from our newest sponsor . . . (Brought to YOU by the Boortean Ambassador)

La-Loo's Whistle-Blowing and Investigative Services

Have you encountered someone attempting to ban or censor books or other bodies of knowledge? Have you witnessed someone destroying back-up systems, flash drives, or other archival memory banks? If so, please contact us so that we can send a team to investigate.

Upon being found guilty, said individuals, depending upon the severity of their deeds, may experience one or more of the following consequences:
- Imprisonment, where they will not be allowed to read.
- Imprisonment where they will be required to read all of the banned books available in our archives.
- Re-education camp.

In extreme situations, said individuals will be sent out the airlock.

Second Place

Omega
Anthony Perconti

This happened at the Heat Death. At the culmination of The Big Chill. My craft limped into The Archive. I had spent several cycles making the journey to the final repository. The stars were extinguished by this point. I didn't see a one twinkling in that vast black. I sank to my knees.

"My people are gone. My world, dead. Final Night is fast approaching," a tear ran down my cheek. "Is there no hope?"

"Stand up." The Archivist waved a hand at the forest of stacks that stretched towards the horizon. He smiled. "Let me tell you a story."

The Future Adventures of
Bailey Belvedere

As the societies of Earth collapse into chaos and destruction, Bailey Belvedere, a U.S. Army Intelligence officer fighting for her very survival, steals aboard an alien spacecraft, and soon finds herself given the authority and power by a superior alien entity to intervene in various problems in the Galaxy. Along the way she frees a world from interstellar slave traffickers, deals with an AI who becomes pregnant, inadvertently destroys a waffle house, fights against the abductors of a special child, and generally finds herself in some sort of trouble from one moment to the next.

Ordering Link:
Print: https://www.hiraethsffh.com/product-page/further-adventures-of-bailey-belvedere-by-tyree-campbell

PDF: https://www.hiraethsffh.com/product-page/further-adventures-of-bailey-belvedere-by-tyree-campbell-1

First Place

Banned Books
Keith Burdon

Kilan sighed as he placed the book on the shelf—the leather worn; the title faded.

"Is that the last one?"

"For now. People will always write..."

"And books will always be lost," chuckled Nort. "All that time, they thought we were abducting humans."

Kilan shrugged. "Sometimes, people just want to believe, even if it's not the truth that is out there."

"What happens to them now?"

"We look after them, of course."

"For how long?"

"Who knows? I guess they might be returned one day." Kilan's eyes narrowed. "But not until the fools on that planet understand their worth."

Honorable Mention

Among the Rain Readers
Tom Gadd

On the planet Okono, water molecules were coded with works of literature so that as you slaked your thirst, you would also be filled with stories or histories or the ideas of philosophers long dead. But when Okono's last civilisation fell and the technology was lost, the water reclaimed its preferred cycles and now, Okono literature exists only as rain, its works fragmented and incomplete, divided among the separate drops. And Okonians must wander beneath storm clouds in hopes of finding the ending of a story or the beginning of a biography or the next line in a love poem.

To the Shore, to the Sea
Erica Ruppert

An alien invasion changes human life on Earth. Their ships disintegrate on Earth, leaking poisons into the soil. The aliens take to the seas. With nowhere for people to go, many perish. Tansy and Luke take their daughter Maria to their family home by the ocean, seeking refuge. But there are strange creatures in the water, and they have a siren's call that is irresistible and unavoidable.

Things change at the shore. Inexplicably, children are hungry all the time. And already it is too late...

To lose a loved one to Death is almost unbearable. But to lose a loved one still living, and changing because of the aliens, requires a surrender no one is prepared to make.

Ordering links:
Print: https://www.hiraethsffh.com/product-page/to-the-shore-to-the-sea-by-erica-ruppert

ePub: https://www.hiraethsffh.com/product-page/to-the-shore-to-the-sea-by-erica-ruppert-2

PDF: https://www.hiraethsffh.com/product-page/to-the-shore-to-the-sea-by-erica-ruppert-1

Galactic Emperor Library 45
Art Gomez

The far-right wing of a collapsed shaft in an abandoned corbomite mine in an undisclosed location is the depository of 45's library. The carefully curated collection contains 45's greatest-hit jobs, hateful screeds, incoherent quotes, turbulent tweets, sexist brags, disloyal enemies list, and rogue's gallery of 45's bootlicking toadies.

45's favorite dictators (evicted from home worlds and exiled to haunt 45 Tower) may peruse the library's contents via the Dark-Web and reminisce to their heartless content.

In order to foil fraudulent journalists and fake historians from vilifying 45, the library, even though the *Greatest Ever*, is never open to the public.

Not Fit for Public Consumption
Lee Clark Zumpe

"These titles are unavailable." The librarian scowled.

"I don't understand," Tanisha said.

"The materials are toxic." Jamaal'ut Sosa, a Shuashoi expat living on Izar, addressed the student in an insolent tone. Sosa, appointed chief librarian of the Terran Heritage Reconstruction Project, loathed off-worlders seeking access to documents. "Ill-intentioned misinformation."

"These aren't political works." Tanisha grew flustered.

"I know what you seek." Sosa folded four upper appendages across his thorax. He clicked his mouthparts, speaking into the translator. "These authors are restricted. Classic Terran literature is deceptive. It depicts unreal realities and impossible outcomes. It is not fit for public consumption."

Wearing Winter Gray
By Lee Clark Zumpe

Atmospheric poetry at its finest is found in Wearing Winter Gray. Lee Clark Zumpe sets his moods and draws forth evocative images and memories, and not a little emotion. Now and then a ray of light shines through his words, so that having created a somber mood, he punctuates it with a bit of joy. Thus it is that Wearing Winter Gray reminds us that Shiny Summer Colors are just around the corner.

Ordering links:
Print: https://www.hiraethsffh.com/product-page/wearing-winter-gray-by-lee-clark-zumpe
ePub: https://www.hiraethsffh.com/product-page/wearing-winter-gray-by-lee-clark-zumpe-2
PDF: https://www.hiraethsffh.com/product-page/wearing-winter-gray-by-lee-clark-zumpe-1

Living Bad Dreams
By Denise Hatfield

When dreams come alive, there's no telling where they will lead. Everything changes when you realize that, dream or no dream, you're going to die. What do you do then?
Print Edition:
https://www.hiraethsffh.com/product-page/living-bad-dreams-by-denise-hatfield-1
ePub Edition:
https://www.hiraethsffh.com/product-page/living-bad-dreams-by-denise-hatfield-2
PDF Edition:
https://www.hiraethsffh.com/product-page/living-bad-dreams-by-denise-hatfield

Widely Read
Greg Schwartz

Jake wandered through the bookstore, unable to find the self-help section. He turned a corner and bumped into a shortish blue creature. The creature glared at Jake.

"Sorry," Jake said. "Are you an alien?"

The creature straightened. "Where I'm from, *you're* the alien."

"What are you doing here?" Jake asked.

"I'm gathering materials for the galaxy's largest library." The creature puffed out its chest. "I'm the Chief Librarian in Charge of Fruit-Based Fiction."

When Jake failed to be impressed, the creature shook its head, grabbed a dozen copies of *James and the Giant Peach*, and stomped off to the register.

Far from Home
Nina D'Arcangela

Muttering to himself, The Keeper shuffled past the conveyer-belt walls as glinting bits of data streamed by. Tasked with finding a suitable recipe for goulash, he wrung his hands, dripping saliva onto the floor from each suckling mouth at the end of his fingers. When the proper glyphs began to appear, The Keeper tapped a foot, the walls halted. Reaching forward, he motioned for the most likely panel to slide out, rotate 90°, and lock into place. Sticking an arm between the crystals, he tasted each one by one, hoping to offer the Earth contingent a small taste of home.

The Drabbun Anthology 2.0
Edited by Francis Wesley Alexander
And t.santitoro

This anthology is perfect for late night bedtime reading.

Print: https://www.hiraethsffh.com/product-page/drabbun-2

PDF: https://www.hiraethsffh.com/product-page/drabbun-2-1

e-Book: https://www.hiraethsffh.com/product-page/drabbun-2-2

Return to Archives
Gary Davis

Veshara shook her head while reading. She was Master Librarian on the most ancient, civilized planet in the galaxy. Her civilization, three billion years old, had visited almost every planet harboring intelligent life in this galaxy. Such populations had by now evolved into permanent states of peace. There was one exception—a small bluish world that residents called Earth. Earthlings had greatly advanced in technology, but with every generation, their wars had cost thousands and then millions more lives. They set a dangerous example for the rest of the galaxy.

Veshara stamped her report on Earth —"Return to Locked Archives."

And a final word by our most-esteemed sponsor . . .(Brought to YOU by the Boortean Ambassador)

T'lar's Re-Education Camp: Watch Out Book Banners!

T'lar hear about book banning and very unhappy. When T'lar's brilliant life partner hear about book banning, she very unhappy. Even worse, podlings cry and cry and cry. They unhappy for all the podlings in the galaxy who can't read books about other histories and cultures and life partners and list goes on. T'lar now work with Cousin La-Loo's Whistle-Blowing and Investigative Services to re-educate book banners and censors and anyone else who encourages podlings and their parental units to avoid exploring. Imagination important. Critical thinking important. Sharing ideas important. T'lar happy to send censors out airlock if won't comply.

END OF TRANSMISSION

www.ingramcontent.com/pod-product-compliance
Lightning Source LLC
LaVergne TN
LVHW021953060526
838201LV00049B/1692